The Dancer of Burton Fair

In the same series:

Wizards and Wampum: Legends of the Iroquois
The Magic Horns: Folk Tales from Africa

Forbes Stuart

The Dancer of Burton Fair

FOLK TALES FROM BRITAIN

Illustrated by Charles Keeping

ABELARD

Text © 1976 Forbes Stuart
Illustrations © 1976 Charles Keeping
First published in Great Britain 1976 by Abelard-Schuman Limited

ISBN 0 200 72460 6

Abelard-Schuman Limited
A Member of the Blackie Group
450 Edgware Road
London W2
Printed in Great Britain by
Thomson Litho Limited, East Kilbride, Scotland

Contents

The Dancer of Burton Fair ___

Devon

"When it comes to dancing," they used to claim in the West Country, "there's nobody can hold a candle to Nelly Wearne of Burton."

Her hair was black, her eyes were green, her figure as trim as Admiral Drake's the *Golden Hind*. In truth, the old Devon seadog himself had once partnered her in the Volta, swearing that only Gloriana herself could match Nelly Wearne in that most intricate of dancing measures.

"I'll take man or devil," Nelly would say (and Frankie Drake was both of those, a man in England and a devil in Spain); and those who saw her dancing carried the memory of it to heaven or hell at the ending of their time in this world. The music came tumbling out of the violin like darting thrushes freed from a wooden cage under the spell of Bob Jethro's magic bow. Faces turned yellow, distorted by shadows in the sputtering light of lanterns placed on the sandy floor of the barn, and the twinkling feet whirled the dust upwards into the rafters.

"She could move so beautifully," they were still recalling many years later, "that no matter how fast she danced, she seemed to have all the time in creation to fashion her graceful steps." Green eyes ablaze in the lanternlight, black hair swirling to match the twirl of her skirt, her arms making lovely patterns, Nelly Wearne in full flight was likened by many a seafarer—not least of them Sir Francis—to the *Golden Hind* scudding proud along Plymouth Sound.

Now, one Midsummer's Day in 1593, just five years after the Spanish Armada had gone down to English guns and Scottish gales, Burton Fair brought its annual hurly-burly to the old town on the cliffs above the sea. Cattle lowed mournfully in the selling enclosures near the whinnying horses caught and tamed on Exmoor, while the silver-tipped clubs of the juggler caught the sunlight, and high above the cobbles the stockinged feet of the acrobat gripped the rope that swayed as he prepared to walk across the sky with the aid of a nine-foot-long balancing pole.

Those looking up at his tottering figure scarcely dared to breathe. Vendors had stopped shouting their wares, and even the dogs that danced on their hind-legs fell silent, resting panting in the dust with lolling tongues. Momentarily, a hush came over Burton Fair, and its bustle froze like a painting.

When the acrobat reached the other side of the street to leap lithely on to the roof of The Bunch of Grapes, the applause came up to him from the market square; and he smiled to hear the copper coins clinking into the metal cup that his young assistant was handing round. Looking down, he saw two figures moving along the cobbled curving street towards Burton Fair.

One of them was short and fat, a dumpling of a man, rolling along with a sailor's gait, preparing his bagpipes for a skirl. His companion, tall and lean, swarthy and handsome with thin black moustache and dark pointed beard, walked as lightly as a cat. He was fashionably dressed, tight-fitted in black, with the sheen of the velvet shimmering in the sunlight and the silver buckles winking on his shoes.

"A popinjay!" the acrobat said to himself. "A dancing master, without a doubt!"

He saw the crowd fall silent again as the first long discordant bagpipe note wailed towards them. When the music accelerated the man in black began dancing on the cobbles, cavorting like a champion. When he stopped, they applauded, and the dancer bowed insolently.

"They told us in the West Indies," he said, "aye, and around the Horn, and even on the other side of America, that the dancers of the West Country were

9

the greatest in the world, but that must be a legend, for we have searched and we can find them not!''

They watched, all of them, as Nelly Wearne stepped out of the front door of The Bunch of Grapes. The acrobat on the rooftop heard her saying with firm confidence in a voice that smouldered, ''I am Nelly Wearne, and I'll take man or devil. And who, pray, Sir, are you?''

The dancing master bowed again, more charming and less insolent now. ''I am Captain Black, Madam, at your service. From my home in East Anglia I have danced up and down the very edges of the world to the music made by my piper and companion here, Sailor Tomkins, who has sailed all seven seas with me. Some call me man and others devil, but only time will tell you who and what I am!''

Burton Fair had never seen such a spectacle of dancing as Captain Black and Nelly Wearne performed that day, on the streets, in field and meadow, on tavern floors and in the long thatched barn which, every Midsummer, witnessed the winding up of Burton Fair. Deep into the night, unflaggingly they danced, looking all the time upon each other with wonderment until only a fool could not have realized that there was love grown between them.

Suddenly, so that everybody was stunned, rain came

pouring down from skies just now bedecked with moon and stars and lightning crackled among the clouds. The thunder exploded like huge rocks clattering down a precipitous mountainside. Gusts of wind hurled the rain against the windows and blew the midnight chimes this way and that, now loud, now soft, as the storm clamour rose and fell.

As the last chimes merged with the tumultuous night, a bolt of lightning zigzagged down the sky and struck the barn. The people of Burton ran screaming from the flames. Wet to the skin, they felt the earth trembling with the thunder, while thatched roof blazed from end to end.

The lightning flashed again to reveal, far below the cliff on which they huddled, a two-masted ship heading out into the boiling Atlantic, its sails filled with the gale that was driving the rain upon them in gouts.

Then, abruptly and inexplicably, the moon and stars were above them, the clouds drawn back, the barn gutted and the fire gone. All was Midsummer calm again. But where was Nelly Wearne?

There was no sign of her. There was no roly-poly piper, and no dapper Captain Black. It was as if the earth had swallowed them. "Or the heavens!" someone whispered fearfully; and others said, "Perhaps they sailed on that mysterious ship?"

The harbourmaster of Burton had no record of any vessel having put out on the last night of the Fair.

In the fifteen years that followed, news of Nelly Wearne trickled through to Burton from the oceans of the world:

"Aye, she married that Captain Black, just as soon as the *Sea Falcon* dropped anchor in the West Indies. Their first boys were twins, and they do say her waist is growing again . . . ."

"Captain Black's a pirate, a privateer like Sir Francis—only he doesn't have the authority of the Queen's licence. Nelly Wearne's his navigator, and a damned good one, they do say, dancing the *Sea Falcon* through shoals and reefs as if born to the sea. They've shovelled in ducats, moidores, and golden guineas too, from merchantmen they've boarded along the trade routes from New Amsterdam right down to the Horn."

"I came across our Nelly in a tavern in Kingston Town. Not more than a year ago it was, as I recall, with summer rosy round the islands. The moon was shining—nearly as strongly as the sun in Devon—over the mango trees, and inside the tavern she and the Captain were footing it nearly as gloriously as the night they disappeared together from Burton on the last night

13

of the Fair. The same fat little fellow was accompanying their whirling on the bagpipes."

During the fifteen years that followed the first fifteen, news of Nelly Wearne became very scarce indeed. Many who had known her were no longer alive. Others had forgotten the lithe young dancer who had vanished with Captain Black thirty years before. But in all her travels through exotic lands, Nelly had never got Burton out of her mind; and as she approached a comely fifty, the yearning to go back home again was constant and intense.

"All right, Nelly, my love," sighed her husband after she had told him a hundred times of her homesickness, "if that's what you want, I'll take you back to where we danced the day we met, and we'll become land-lubbers again."

"But the ship?" she asked. "What will you do with the *Sea Falcon*?"

"Bequeath it to the crew," he replied with the promptness of a man who has given a matter some thought, "and the lads can choose their new captain themselves. Our sons are too respectable to follow in our footsteps, Nelly. One schoolmaster, two farmers, and Tom a lawyer in Jamestown. He's the one who came closest to being a privateer like his father. Not a pirate among the four of them, but good lads withal,

14

I'll grant you that."

"And when we're settled near Burton, they could perhaps visit us with their families from time to time," she said wistfully. "Or," she continued brightly, "we could go and see them!"

"But one way or the other," her husband concluded, "we'll have to change our names when we go home, Nelly, for there's a price on our heads and I have no wish to swing at Tyburn Way for piracy. God knows I love dancing still, but not at the end of a rope, with the crowds on the grandstands gawping at our going!"

It was thirty years later almost to the day she had vanished so dramatically in smoke and flame, that Nelly Wearne came back to her childhood haunts. Again, it was Midsummer, stars and moon clear against a cloudless sky, with scarcely a ripple to ruffle the black sea as the ship glided towards Falmouth, not more than half a day's brisk walk from Burton.

Clouds came, as they had done thirty years before, to choke the light of the moon. Thunder rumbled across the suddenly agitated water, lightning speared the foam; and the rowing-boat bringing Nelly home at last rocked on the waves and wallowed in the troughs. On the clifftop high above the sea, lightning struck a thatch-roofed barn which roared into flame to guide the seafarers into a sheltered cove.

"Goodbye, Nelly," shouted Captain Black above the tumult of the storm. "I'll be with you in a few months when I've settled our affairs."

"Take care of yourself, Edward!" she cried, stepping on to the beach. One of the sailors pushed the boat back into the deep water before leaping aboard again. Waving farewell, she watched the dinghy's erratic course until it merged with the darkness. Then she trudged up the steep, slippery path leading to the Widow Trethowan's cottage on the top of the cliff.

She turned to gaze down at the sea, now far below her, and at that very moment, a huge jagged fork of lightning lit up the seething waters to reveal a two-masted vessel dashing against the rocks. Then all was dark again, and she was sick with horror and dismay. But she shook her head and said firmly to herself, "I shall not believe that Edward my husband perished tonight, until it is presented to me as a fact. Even then I shan't accept it until the fact itself is verified."

She moved into the Widow Trethowan's cottage as Mrs Whitefield. She slept but fitfully that first night. As soon as it was dawn she hurried to the cliff's edge and looked down on the tranquil sea, There was no sign of wreckage, not a snapped-off mast, nor a spar, nor a staved-in rowing boat. Her fears began to quieten and she wondered how much time would pass before she

16

would have definite news of her husband.

While she waited, she earned some extra money by setting herself up as a fortune-teller, bringing much happiness to those who, in return for crossing her palm with silver, were rewarded with predictions of future well-being and joy.

Nobody suspected who the stranger really was although they talked about her a great deal in that small community; but one old biddy was heard to say, shaking her head reminiscently the while, that "she brings me in mind of Nelly Wearne that was, long before your time, my dearies. She was the greatest dancer in these parts. Disappeared from Burton Fair, on the last night of it, in a storm with Captain Black the pirate. Thirty years ago, if it was a day. You should have seen them dancing together to the bagpipe's tune, marvellous it was, I'm telling you now!"

A year dragged by, and a further three months, before a fat little seaman with rolling gait rapped at the door of the Widow Trethowan's cottage.

"Sailor Tomkins!" she cried as they embraced, he smirking like a cat that has left no cream in the saucer, and her tears wetting his shining bald head. Then she stepped back, serious and concerned now. "Are they alive? The truth now, mind! No hanky-panky, no shilly-shallying, please!"

17

"Alive and flourishing," he replied promptly, "and I speak as Captain Black's messenger, his bearer of good tidings, as you might say, Ma'am."

"But how did you get here?" she asked. "And where is he, and why has it been so long, and is there news of my sons?"

"Sit down, Nelly Wearne," he said soothingly, "and I'll answer your questions one by one, from the very beginning."

She listened enthralled as he described how their ship had been dashed on the Falmouth rocks to sink without trace, "but not before we had all managed to scramble into the boats and row away. The sea turned calm for us, although lightning and thunder continued and the clouds still covered the moon.

"Then the clouds parted, and a trail of moonlight led us to a ship anchored out in the bay. Her sails were furled, and it was so quiet that we knew most of the crew must have been carousing ashore. When we stopped rowing, we could actually hear the snores of the look-out coming from the crow's nest."

He told her how they had taken the ship without a fight, sending the skeleton crew ashore in a rowing boat. "Then we set sail immediately for the West Indies, plundering three fat merchantmen along the way. As soon as we dropped anchor in Kingston, the Captain

18

bade me work my passage back to England and bring you news of the family. Your boys are hearty and prospering." And he gave Nelly Wearne news of children and grandchildren as well.

She sighed, "And when will the Captain be joining his lonely wife in Devon, would you be saying?"

"Captain Black is busy recouping the losses sustained when the *Sea Falcon* went down," he replied gravely, "and it is my considered opinion that he'll be with you long before another year is up."

She clapped her hands in delight. "You have made me very happy," she said, "but tell me, old friend, what will you be doing now?"

"I'll find a ship somewhere along the coast," he said. "I am not ready to be a landlubber yet. And in the course of time I'll return to settle here with you and the Captain, ma'am. So it's goodbye, then, until our next meeting."

But it was not exactly as Sailor Tomkins had predicted. A whole year went by, and then another six months. It wasn't until springtime brought the crocuses and daffodils, nodding yellow on the meadow's green, and chestnuts flowered and birds shrilled in the dawning, that Edward Black and his wife Nelly were reunited in the Widow Trethowan's cottage.

"What kept you so long?" she asked him, and he

related how they had "boarded one last ship on the way home, just for old time's sake, you know how it was. The crew we captured were mutineers who had made their skipper walk the plank because, they claimed, he had been a tyrant over them. They offered to show us where treasure was buried that would make us all rich beyond the dreams of avarice. They had the map which their captain had kept to himself to his cost. So what could we do, Nelly dear, I ask you as one privateer to another, eh?"

He told her how they had sailed back to the West Indies and how, on a tiny isolated island—"little larger than Burton Fair"—the parchment had led them to a spot where their spades struck metal and they had hauled out three iron cases. When they prised them open, the display of jewels had been so dazzling that the very sun paled in comparison.

"So we are rich, Nelly and we can live as we please as long as we like, never wanting for anything at all. I'm giving the ship to the men, as I promised long ago, and now I'm a retired sea captain putting his feet up gracefully in slippered ease."

But a lifetime's habits die hard, and as summer gave way to winter, the rain pattering on the roof day after day, fog hiding the sea and nothing to do except toast muffins in front of the fire, the mantle of boredom

20

began to descend upon Captain Edward Whitefield. It had enshrouded him completely by the time the crocuses danced on the hillsides again and the birds, back from their sojourn in the warm south, were trilling and twittering of one horizon giving way to another, and yet another, and another one after that.

He hurled his slippers at the fireplace. "I am too old to dance on land," he bellowed, "but I can still lead them a pretty dance on the open sea, Nelly. I am bored to distraction, the old life calls to me again, but I'll make a compromise in my mature years for both our sakes. Instead of returning to piracy, I'll become a smuggler, and this house of ours will be my base. What do you say, girl? Without the excitement of some nefarious enterprise, I shall curl up and die."

"I have never sought to curb you, Edward," replied Nelly with a sigh, "and I shall not start doing so now. If you must dance again, on land or at sea, so let it be."

Soon Captain Black, his jetblack beard flecked now with grey, was back in business, master of a small and highly manoeuverable ship with a hand-picked crew, men who returned to their homes on the coast after every short trip across the Channel that brought them back with barrels of cognac, rolls of silk, and caskets of jewels. Their ship was berthed in a cove known only to themselves and to the landlubbers who took the goods off their hands at the end of every voyage.

Then it was winter again. A blanket of gloom spread upon the world, bringing fogs and high seas and gales that propelled the waves across the Atlantic to crash upon the Devon rocks. Captain Black's ship could not put to sea in such foul weather, and a fortnight of enforced inactivity was too much for the retired privateer.

Sailor Tomkins had returned to England to join his Captain just before that fateful winter began. For the rest of his days, he never again had to buy a drink. Whenever he called in at an inn or a tavern in Devon or Cornwall, someone would pour the roly-poly pudding of a man a liberal measure of rum and ask him to tell the assembly about Captain Black's last moments in this world:

"That last fortnight of enforced leisure really did for the Captain, who was always a man of action. Boredom was heavy upon him, and on the fourteenth day in the sheltered cove, with the storm still raging outside, he went berserk, ordering the gunner to shoot holes in the grey low-slung clouds. The guns boomed again and again while Captain Black cavorted on the deck, shaking his fist at the clouds and cursing the Devil himself for a fool and an impostor. Suddenly, as if the heavens were replying to the cannonade and the curses,

thunder rolled and a bolt of lightning rammed down the skies straight at the Captain. As God is my witness, he burst into flame and disappeared. Only the smoke hovered above his bundle of clothes that lay on the deck where he had been standing."

At exactly the same moment that Captain Black disappeared in smoke and flame, lightning took hold of the thatched roof of the Widow Trethowan's cottage, which roared into flames and burned to the ground before neighbours could even struggle through the gale to reach it.

Within minutes of Captain Black's translation by fire and the gutting of Nelly's cottage, the sea grew calm and the sun came out while the clouds fled to the four corners of the heavens. All that survived, lying dishevelled on the cottage floor, was a bundle of clothes that Nelly had been seen wearing that very morning.

When an inquest was held, it came out that Mr and Mrs Whitefield were in reality Captain Black and his wife Nelly Wearne. The old biddy who gave evidence at the inquest could remember as far back as the day that Captain Black and dancing Nelly Wearne had left Burton Fair, nearly forty years before, vanishing as a barn blazed from end to end in the storm that came raging out of nowhere. And she recalled the ghostly ship that had sailed away on that dramatic night in 1593.

24

"It is my belief," she concluded gravely, "that Captain Edward Black was in league with the Devil. When he offended his master by his insults, he was taken away in smoke and flame by Old Nick, and Nelly Wearne with him, for she had consorted with him for more than thirty years."

From that day to this, in every corner of Devon, nobody has come forward to challenge the old lady's judgement. Nor have the people there forgotten the marvellous prowess of Nelly Wearne and Captain Black in the four centuries that have passed since they danced, on the streets, in field and meadow, on tavern floors, and in the long thatched barn which, every Midsummer, witnessed the winding up of Burton Fair.

Trooper Thompson's Banquet

Westmoreland

Only three men remained near the freshly filled grave, covered with the flowers strewn there by the old lady's relatives. The gravestone shadows were lengthening in the early evening, and from the chimneys in the village houses cooking smells mingled with the grey smoke that poured into the sky.

"The old woman had a long life, indeed," mused Corporal Blackstone (who had fought at Malplaquet and Oudenarde with General Marlborough), "and lucky enough she was, to have spent less than half of it under the Hanoverian yoke." Then he read aloud the inscription on her tombstone: "Ada Wheatshaft, departed this life on 4th July 1752, aged 82 years, mourned by all."

"Aye, a long life and, more important, a good one," responded the Reverend Alan Hargreaves, the shepherd of his Westmoreland flock for more than thirty years. "Two of her sons died in the Stuart cause at Culloden not more than seven years ago now, going north to volunteer and they not even Scotsmen."

Young George Kitchen stooped down to pick up a skull that had been unearthed earlier in the day by the gravediggers and had been hidden behind a gravestone in order not to offend the mourners. "Who was this, then, I wonder?" he queried, insolent at seventeen in the company of his elders.

"Judging from where it was found," offered the Corporal, "it's the skull of Trooper Thompson who fought like me, wi' Marlborough in the dear days when English kings were Englishmen and Queen Anne was on the throne. Thompson was a cantankerous fellow, though, always in some scrape or another, and he hasn't found his final peace after all these years."

A blackbird fluttered by overhead as he concluded: "His troubled spirit often returns, and it would not surprise me if Trooper Thompson were listening to us at this very moment from the other side of the grave."

"Do you mean to tell us," asked young Kitchen, "that because he cannot rest, he comes as a ghost or a spirit to disturb the good citizens of Kirkby Malhamdale?" And with that, he dropped the skull and kicked it rolling among the gravestones.

"You wouldn't do that again to an old soldier of the Queen!" snapped Corporal Blackstone with some heat. George Kitchen's reply was to boot the skull again. It clattered against a gravestone, leering at the three men.

27

The clergyman did no more than sigh with the sadness of a man who knows how much opposition there is to God's word upon this earth, particularly among his own parishioners. But the Corporal spoke sharply to the boy: "Say after me, churlish lout, if you dare, the words that will invite the owner of this skull to meet you here at midnight and call you to a banquet that his bony fingers will spread on this moss-covered green stone here."

George Kitchen hesitated, as well he might. But his own bravado had committed him to action. So, in a clear voice without a tremor, gazing the while at Trooper Thompson's toothless jaws and sockets where eyeballs once swivelled he recited after the Corporal:

Are you good or are you devil?
Are you ghost or imp so evil?
For I with neither fright nor fear,
Will come to share your midnight cheer.

It was said, and forgotten—at least, by George Kitchen. When he went to bed around ten o' clock that evening, he was asleep almost as soon as his head touched the pillow. But not for long.

The crackling sound of small stones striking the wooden casement just above his head stirred him into wakefulness. He heard a voice singing, each wavering note as watery as if it had bubbled up from the very floor of the ocean. He listened, not frightened but somewhat apprehensive:

When midnight's tolled
Food will be cold
Upon the green gravestone.

Where is my guest?
I cannot rest!
I shall not dine alone.

George Kitchen, come, without delay,
For we must dine before the day
Can affright
The night
And drive the dark away!

By now there *was* some fear in him, and he felt the hair rising on his head, but to stop the stones clattering against the shutters, he cried out as calmly as he was able, "All right, whoever you are, I am awake now. Hold on a minute, will you?"

The singing stopped, and the flying stones. He pushed open the casement to let in the moonlight and noticed the clouds converging on the moon as he looked out and saw his host.

Silent now, Trooper Thompson stood before him,

dressed in a uniform gone mouldy and mildewed. His face was as green as the moss-green gravestone that would serve as table at the feast. There were holes where his eyes should have been, and around him an aura of decay, like one who keeps on dying but is never properly dead.

George Kitchen was shivering now, and his voice quivered as he spoke to the apparition: "Go back to the graveyard, I pray you, and I shall dress and join you presently."

Without a sound, the figure turned slowly and dissolved into the night. Within a few minutes, George Kitchen was rapping urgently at the Reverend Alan Hargraves's door which was opened by the clergyman who said in greeting, "I presume the ghost of Trooper Thompson has paid a call upon you and now you're importuning my aid."

"Yes, sir," replied George in new-found humility, and went inside to relate the midnight happenings to God's representative at Kirby Malhamdale.

"You're a bad lad," the clergyman upbraided him very gently, "and you have brought all this unpleasantness upon your own head by your blaspheming. But you are, after all, a Christian (or were baptised as one in this parish by myself, God help me!) so I suppose I shall have to help you in your self-inflicted plight.

First, we shall pray on our knees for God's guidance and then we shall beard the ghost."

As the churchyard gate creaked behind them, the bells in the square stone tower began to chime, although nobody was inside to pull on the ropes that made them peal. The clouds by now had reached the moon, and darkness came like a snuffing of the candle of the night.

"Am I dreaming?" George whispered, knowing full well that he was not, gazing aghast at Trooper Thompson's tormented spirit luminously moving, weaving wraithlike, as quiet as smoke, in and out among the gravestones.

The Trooper stopped when George's faltering voice enquired whether he minded *two* guests, even if he had only invited one. His reply, rusty and echoing, seemed to emerge from a sepulchre: "It was not what I expected, nor what I wished, but never mind, we are all Christian souls together, and there's food enough for three and more on the cold gravestone. Come, let us dine. The victuals are cold but very good."

Again he raised his quavering voice in song:

The banquet is spread
Here where the dead
In their coffins sleep
Dark and Deep

Where bodies moulder
Growing older.
One day that will be your fate!
But, come, eat now,
It's growing late.

"Before we even touch the food," said the Reverend Hargreaves, "I must say Grace. We are, as you rightly observed, all Christians gathered together, the living and the dead, so there can be no possible objection to a prayer of gratitude being offered up as a prelude to the meal."

Hardly had he started than the Trooper began to move agitatedly, in and out among the gravestones, up in the air and down again, crying passionately, "Stop! Stop, I say! What you are mouthing there is a Protestant Grace, and I was always a Catholic, buried here in a Protestant churchyard because of the hazards of practising the true religion in blaspheming England when I was a man alive. But *my* Grace comes neither from Rome nor from Canterbury. Listen! Listen!"

Now the churchbells clanged and jangled with supernatural speed. Darkness and blinding light alternated in the church as if the very stones were in torment. The organ notes rose to an ear-numbing crescendo while an invisible choir screamed De Profundis with a satanic shrillness and cacophony. A swarm of bats streamed out of the square tower, the flapping of their wings heralding a gale that blew the dissident spirits clean away.

Silence prevailed again in the gloomy churchyard.

"Now *that* is what I call a Grace," murmured Trooper Thompson appreciatively, "a blessing on the meal, indeed. Come, let us eat now."

George Kitchen would never forget what happened next.

"Would you mind passing me the *salt*, there's a good fellow?" he heard the clergyman enquire amiably of the ghost.

Mention of that common condiment immediately banished Trooper Thompson. One second he was there, the next he was gone. At the same time the banquet dishes vanished from the green gravestone. The clouds that clung to the moon disappeared and they were all but dazzled by the illumination it cast upon them in the graveyard, now as still and quiet as the bodies mouldering under the gravestones.

The demented spirit of Trooper Thompson must have found tranquility at last, for since that July night in 1752 his ghost has never again come back to haunt the villagers of Kirkby Malhamdale.

Jovial Brother Jucundus

Even the ear-splitting cacophony of the Fair that turned York on its head once a year on Easter Monday did not interfere with the inflexible monastic routine that prevailed at the Priory of St Leonards. The monks were in their cells, sleeping from one o'clock to two, as they had done every day during the three centuries that had passed since the founding of their order in 1210.

But one monk lay awake, twisting and turning on his pallet, tormented by the muffled jangle of Easter Fair which penetrated the thick stone walls of the church.

Brother Jucundus, beset by memories of more uproarious times, groaned in his misery. "How scraggy I have become beneath these dull grey robes! Where is the round fat belly that used to know tripe by the basinful, fat pork chops done to a turn, and puddings as big as a man's head? Where are the jests and songs and tankards of flowing ale?"

His mind raced backwards a year, to 1509, and he saw himself at the banquet which had commemorated the crowning of the new King, Henry VIII, and had changed his life. He had, as usual, eaten too much and drunk too copiously of wine and beer; and on the following day, in pain and remorse and sickened by constant debauchery, he had taken holy vows, to become Brother Jucundus the monk, existing on vegetables and bread and barely enough beer with his meals to wet his tongue.

"I can't stand it any longer!" he hissed through clenched teeth. "I made a bad decision when I was neither well nor sober, and if I do not smash the shackles of restraint I shall go mad." Rising to his feet and tucking his wooden sandals under his arm, he walked furtively into the chapel to steal a crown from the iron-bound collection-box, and lifted the big key from its hook on the vestry wall. He unlocked the door, leaving it open while he slipped his feet into his sandals, and clattered down the cobbled lane, past the Gothic magnificence of York Minster that overlooked the market square, seething with the tumult of Easter Fair.

Wild-eyed, he revelled in the jumble of colours and sounds, the jostling crowds of pleasure-seekers regaled by the vendors' cries of "Come buy! Come buy!" Fiddles clashed with the bagpipe's squeal, drums rattled and rumbled and the blast from the horns was as brassy as the spring sun's beneficence. His long-repressed appetites and emotions burst their bonds, and Brother

Jucundus embraced the Easter Fair with the unrestrained fervour of a suitor who meets his lover again after enforced separation and knows that the reunion will be a brief one.

Afterwards, his recollection would be a phantasmagoria of citizens laughing and shouting, tethered bears snarling at their baiters, dogs, resplendent with ruffs, dancing grotesquely on their hindlegs, and a giant who towered over child-voiced dwarfs and snapped a thick chain by expanding his vast and hairy chest. In a frenzy of excess, the liberated monk guzzled the gingerbread cakes, the greasy pies, and the meat that came red and dripping from the spit. Tankard after foaming tankard of ale splashed into his insatiable stomach.

There would be a pandemonium of memories—up and down, up and down, the dizzy dip of the swings, the fairground reeling about the whirli-go-round, music blaring, citizens shrieking, the sun beaming, and always the froth-topped tankards of beer.

The bell of St Leonards chimed two, calling the monks from their cells to devotions in the chapel. The churchdoor stood ajar, the key in the lock; the solitary crown that had graced the collection box had gone, and Brother Jucundus was missing! Affronted, the Prior uttered his terse commandment: "Brother Cedric, Brother Benjamin, I want you to scour the town for our erring brother. But go first to the Fair. I fear you may find him there, disgracing St Leonards and covering our reputation for piety with the shadow of doubt." They swept down the cobbled lane towards the jangling sounds in the Market square.

Abstemious and fastidious fellows both, they could hear their fallen brother even before they saw him, and they shuddered distastefully at the sound of his drunken voice bellowing and slobbering above the strident discord of the Easter Fair:

In dulce jubilo,
Up, up, up we go!

They found him riding on the see-saw boat, tankard in hand, his grey robes besmirched with dust and dirt. They pushed their way through the spectators who had gathered to hoot with laughter at the undignified antics of the jovial monk. Regarding Brothers Cedric and Benjamin through eyes now glazed and bloodshot, Brother Jucundus tumbled out of the see-saw boat, picked himself up from the ground and staggered over to his stern-visaged fellow-monks while he continued bellowing raucously:

In dulce jubilo,
Up, up, up we go!

Citizens on their way to the Fair that afternoon were startled to behold two monks, perspiring and scarlet with embarrassment, pushing a wheelbarrow containing a sprawling monk whose eyes were closed blissfully while he roared, over and over, "In dulce jubilo!" The Prior and his brethren were tight-lipped with suppressed fury when Brother Jucundus was wheeled into the Priory, too far gone to get to his feet, too drunk even to know where he was. The refrain of his song boomed and echoed in the chapel:

In dulce jubilo,
Up, up, up we go!

Comatose in his drunken stupor, Brother Jucundus began to snore, deaf to the emotionless voice of his superior and unaware that he was being tried and convicted for behaviour so blasphemous as to call for the supreme penalty: "Jucundus, you are condemned to be walled up alive in a niche in the cellar of St Leonards. And may God have mercy on your soul."

They propped him up against the cellar wall, placing a jug of water and a crust of bread at his feet; and after three monks had mixed the mortar and laid one brick upon another, the Prior himself pushed the very last brick into position, walling Jucundus into the niche that was now his tomb. As they trooped up the cellar

39

steps, leaving their errant brother to his doom, they could hear his voice fading while he continued to sing drunkenly:

In dulce jubilo,
Up, up, up we go!

His head throbbing with spasms of pain, the monk awoke in utter darkness and sobered up with astonishing swiftness when his groping hands encountered walls all around him. "I'm bottled up and left to die!" he gasped, knowing that he would soon perish for lack of air.

Pressing his back against one wall and his feet against the other, he pushed and strained, desperation giving him strength. Suddenly he felt himself falling outwards and rolling over with dislodged bricks crashing about him. Dazed by his exertions and weakened by the after-effects of his riotous afternoon, he lay still for a while to collect his senses.

He was in a cellar, and he had emerged from a bricked-up niche. That much was clear. When his bemused brain cleared, he realised where he was—in the cellar belonging to the Priory of St Mary's, which he recalled was so close to St Leonards that only a wall divided the basements of the two monasteries. In the gloom he could make out the rows of trestles supporting barrels of Malmsey wine. He shuddered.

41

"Never again," he whispered fervently, "never again, not in a thousand years!"

He knew that the monks of St Mary's were members of the Cistercian Order whose vow of silence was broken only once a year, on Easter Monday. "That means they'll be silent again later tonight," he thought, "so I can fit in upstairs with nobody to question me. And St Leonards will go on believing that I died on the day of York Fair, walled up in a niche down in the cellar with only a jug of water and a crust of bread to see me along the way to eternity—as fine an example of man's inhumanity to man as I have ever encountered."

So he moved into a routine even duller than the one he had known next door, sleeping in the communal dormitory, finding an empty place at the meagre table, and chanting plain-song with the other monks, the ban on human utterance extending to everything except singing in unison. But he was alive at least, and grateful for that, and he managed to stifle his yearning to carouse in the world that lay waiting outside the priory door. The year dragged its feet, and time was a tortoise.

And then one day he heard again the bedlam of Easter Fair—shrilling flutes and trumpet blare, and the stall-keepers crying to the surging crowds: "Pies to eat! Pork hot from the spit! Good ale! Good ale!" He could *feel* the exhilarating dip of the swings and the dizzy spinning of the whirli-go-round, the warmth of the sun and human communion. Pies and pork chops swam past his eyes, with a bowlful of swilling tripe and onions and limitless tankards of ale.

But the reality was the dormitory filled with the rumbling snores of the monks having their afternoon sleep. "No, I cannot," he whispered to himself. "I dare not go out now because of what happened to me one year ago." Then he smiled. "But who could take offence If I went down to the cellar and sampled the beer and Malmsey in such tiny quantities that nobody would be aware of my insignificant transgression?"

So quietly that not one of the sleeping monks so much as stirred, he rose from his pallet on the floor and descended into the gloomy cellar like a shadow.

That evening the monks were as garrulous as washer-women, making the most of the one day that sanctioned the breaking of their year-long silence. They shouted to each other across the long refrectory table, some laughing immoderately, until the Prior clanked his mug on the scrubbed table-top and asked, "Where is Brother Jucundus whose turn it is to fetch our beer today? Brother Simon, go into the cellar and see what is keeping our brother." The hubbub of converse rose again, and some of the monks banged their mugs on the table and bellowed, "Beer! Beer!" until the Prior silenced them with a withering glance.

Brother Simon's lantern threw his shadow flickering on the wall as he went carefully down the steps into the dark cellar. His sandals slopped on the stone floor which was awash with beer, and the rich red Malmsey wine reserved for important visitors—such as Kings and Archbishops—was splashing on the ground from the opened spigot. He raised his lantern. Brother Jucundus was sitting astride a barrel, a mug in each hand, and as he perceived Brother Simon, he began to roar a rollicking song:

In dulce jubilo,
Up, up, up we go!

Too befuddled to know, too drunk to care, Brother Jucundus went on singing while the Prior condemned him to be walled up alive exactly where he had burst out of his niche in a flurry of falling bricks precisely one year before. His raucous bellowing was muffled by the Prior's pushing the last brick securely into position, and the monks trooped up the cellar steps, leaving their errant brother to his doom.

At that very moment a monk came down the steps to the cellar from the adjoining St Leonards to pour the beer for the Easter Monday evening meal. What

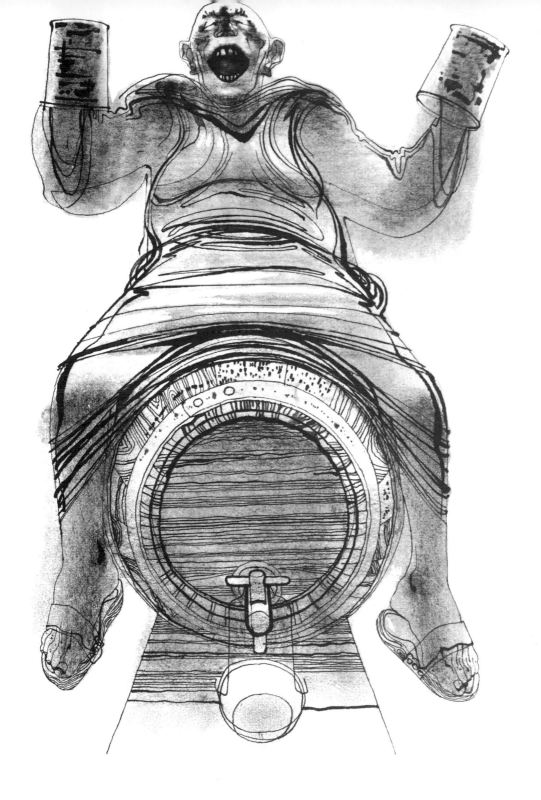

he heard, sent him scurrying upstairs to the refrectory, to stand mad-eyed and panting like a man who had seen a ghost with its head under its arm.

"A miracle on this holy day!" he proclaimed to the assembled monks, crossing himself hastily. "It's Brother Jucundus returned from the grave, a year to the day since we sealed him in his tomb. He lives again, and is singing as lustily as ever!"

In confusion, consternation, and a measure of disbelief, the Prior and his monks swarmed down the steps into the cellar, to hear the familiar voice of Brother Jucundus shouting out the song they remembered so well:

In dulce jubilo,
Up, up, up we go!

"Tear down the wall!" commanded the ashen-visaged Prior, and crowbars brought the bricks crashing down to reveal Brother Jucundus, sobering now, the crust of bread and jug of water standing untouched at his feet. Blinking his eyes in the candle-light and smiling wanly, he said with fervent gratitude: "In dulce jubilo!"

Reinstated and welcomed back into the fraternity, Brother Jucundus was to prosper in the course of the years, donning the Prior's robes and by his good works becoming renowned throughout York as "Saint Jucundus our head and father". Unrepenting and unreformed—but never again embracing excess as he had done on that fateful Easter Monday of 1510—he illumined the austere gloom of St Leonards with joviality and conviviality.

In the twenty years that followed his elevation, growing ever more rotund and twinkle-eyed, he and his band of brothers were always welcome in the inns and taverns of York. They became a much-loved institution at Easter Fair, carousing and roistering but never violating the frontier that lies between moderation and intemperance; and every Easter Monday the crowds congregated to watch the holy men riding on the see-saw boat and singing the words that would forever be associated with Brother Jucundus:

In dulce jubilo,
Up, up, up we go!

But they did not neglect the serious area of their calling; and when Brother Jucundus died, to be buried on Easter Monday 1537, delaying the opening of the Fair he loved so well, every able-bodied citizen of York walked behind his coffin in the longest funeral procession in the town's entire history. Even before the first flowers rose from the sods that covered his grave to

47

smile at the sun, the Reformation wrought its profound changes, and King Henry VIII issued the Decree that closed the priories and monasteries from one end of England to the other and confiscated the wealth of the Church.

In many parts of England the discomforture heaped upon the clerics was greeted with cheers of approval, but in York there was sadness when the Priory of St Leonards closed its doors. And for many years afterwards, the wreaths and bouquets of remembrance were piled high every Easter Monday on the grave of jovial Brother Jucundus.

The Worm of Lambton Hall

Durham

When Richard the First was England's King, called
by the people *The Lion-Hearted* or *Coeur de Lion* (for
French was the language of the court, and English the
bastard tongue of the commoners), he was so consumed
by a lusting after battle that fighting kept him out of
Westminster Palace for all but six months of his reign.
The Holy Crusades sent Richard and his Christian
armies rampaging through Europe to put the Infidel to
the sword in Jerusalem itself.

Almost every noble house in England sent one strap-
ping son to prove his manhood in battle, pillage and
plunder; and with each knight went a serf or two, to
wash and dress his master, run his errands and cook
his food. But the heir to Lambton Hall in County Durham made no move to join in the holy carnage and,
what is more, he seemed to go out of his way to offend
his neighbours. They represented the new aristocracy
of England whose titles had stemmed from the Domes-
day Book little more than a hundred years before, at
the end of William the Conqueror's subjugation of this

49

island which had laid waste the greater part of Yorkshire and Durham.

What the serfs in their hovels thought about their young master was of little account, for a serf only thought what was put into his head by those more highly placed than himself. His opinions wouldn't matter a jot until 1381 when they would all but topple young Richard II from his throne; but at Lambton Hall, eight years before the twelfth century came to an end, the serfs were saying of their young master: "He's uncouth and earthy, with a fine command of coarse language; and if fate hadn't made him a lord, he'd surely have been one of us."

His neighbours took a different view of his rough and dissolute ways. "On our walk to the House of the Lord on a Sunday morning, we can observe him crossing the bridge to fish in the River Wear, a deliberate affront to our religious sensibilities. As we approach, the fellow commences cursing and swearing no better than a serf, ostensibly shouting abuse at the fish who refuse to rise to his bait, but in reality it was done to offend us. He loves to see the ladies blushing to the base of their necks. It's high time he went to the Crusades, for unlike some of us who are too cultivated and sensitive to carry sword and shield, he is strong and healthy and rather lacking in imagination, and the war will make a better man of him."

But as the Crusades dragged on, with Richard and his allies putting Constantinople to sword and flame, the greatest library in the world going up in smoke and flame at Alexandria, young Lambton made not the slightest move towards buckling on his sword and committing himself to every able-bodied young man's desire. He jousted effectively but perfunctorily; and to his own father—without a wife since she had died when her son was only five—he was so matter-of-fact that when they dined at the long oak table glistening with silver plate, they would not say a word to each other from one meal to the next.

"There's good in the boy," his father confided to an old friend, "but no way of bringing it out. It is as if he will do nothing until Destiny beckons, so all we can do is wait and see."

One Sunday morning in October when the clouded sky was turning the swollen waters grey and the church-bell on the other side of the forest called the devout to prayers, a fierce tug at the young man's line all but dragged him into the river. The passers-by were scalded by the obscenity of his invective as he struggled on the bank to land his catch, and the damsels blushed all the way down to their palpitating bosoms, unconcealed by their church-going gowns.

51

After they had scampered away the struggle continued, the water foaming and frothing until at last the fish at the end of the line went limp. The young man managed to haul in his catch after a two-hour battle, landing it just as his neighbours passed by again on their way back from the church service.

It was the ugliest and biggest worm he had ever seen, six feet in length with nine holes along each side of its head. "I've caught the Devil himself!" he cried in disgust, finding the small-scale monster so repulsive that he dragged the worm across to a nearby well, which was no longer in use, and bundled it over the stone lip while his neighbours averted their gaze, the ladies affecting to hold their hands before their horrified eyes but in reality peering fascinated through the interstices of their fingers. He heard the dull splash far below as it hit the slimy water.

Shortly afterwards, nobody knew why or how, the young heir to Lambton Hall became more gentle in his manners and less uncouth in his speech, although young damsels continued to blush scarlet in his handsome presence, even when he didn't utter a syllable; and he spoke more often and warmly with his lonely father. He spent more time on his knees in the chapel and, spiritually refreshed, he would joust with a concentration and vigour so fierce that his trainer was betimes

terrified. It was clear that Destiny was working its way with him.

The change in him became so apparent to all that nobody was surprised when he announced his intention of joining the Crusades and, taking one of his father's servants with him, rode away across the wooden bridge that spanned the River Wear.

Meanwhile, down in the well near the bridge, the ugly worm (which had been more alive than it had seemed) was flourishing in the filthy water and growing fatter and longer by the day until its very size squeezed it out over the lip of the well. It wriggled into the river and coiled itself around a huge rock that stood in the water about thirty feet—or the length of the worm at that point in its growing—from the bank where young Lambton had spent so much time fishing before his departure for the Holy Land.

Up and down the river, fishermen trolled with a diminishing rate of success until they were fishing simply for the philosophy of it. Not a single fish splashed and glided in the water, while the worm grew longer until its coils completely covered what would come to be known in the course of the centuries as Worm Rock.

"That worm has been gorging itself on the fish till there are none left," complained Lord Lambton's neighbours. "It's young Lambton that's to blame, and

Holy Crusade or no, his father should be called upon to make recompense by stocking a big pond with fingerlings in a place where the monster doesn't wander, so that the ancient sport can be revived."

The serfs in their hovels had other cause for ire. "We used to get food from the river; but now that the fish are gone, are we getting a single penny more for our labouring to compensate us for our loss? *We* cannot afford to fish for pleasure—not that they allow us much time for that! But what will happen to our food supply when the monster's appetite increases with its growing?"

What occurred next was on a small and unheroic scale. When a farmer found that one sheep was missing from his flock, he went looking for it. While he was searching, he came across a deep slimy trail furrowed in the ground that led to the riverbank. Curled round its rock, the monster was sleeping off its meal of uncooked mutton. Word of this flashed through the small community, and a special weekday service was held to petition God's intervention. The nobility occupied their private pews, with their names emblazoned on them, in the front of the nave nearest to the pulpit, while the common people sat in their allocated places at the back of the chapel. Because the service was in Latin, nobody understood much of what was being said, for the gentry conversed in French while the serfs spoke English; but they could feel the emotion of it, and absolute unanimity prevailed in the class-divided chapel as everybody prayed for an end to the growing monster whose continuing robust health was of deep concern to all members of the community.

When Sunday came a few days later, and the clanging of the bells called the people to church, they were overjoyed to find the rock in the river shiny with slime and unencumbered by the massive worm. "Our prayers have been heeded," they said. "The curse has been lifted from our backs. The devil-worm has gone, down the river and away to the open sea. Now the fish will return, and we shall not fear for our sheep and cattle."

But joy gave way to sudden despair and shock when the last prayer released them from their Sunday observances.

The farmer who had lost a sheep was the first to notice that something was amiss. "My flock!" he cried. "It's half the size it was this morning. Where are my sheep and lambs? I am ruined if I do not find them." The people stopped in their tracks at this outburst, and they groaned in dismay as he pointed across the meadow. "There's your worm!" he shouted bitterly. "A curse on young Lambton for going overseas to the wars and leaving us to bear the brunt of his iniquity!"

56

Coiled three times round the hill in the very middle of the fields, the monster was at rest. The bones and wool of the sheep he had torn to pieces were all around him. And that was only the beginning of the terror. The worm began to devour lambs at all times of the day and night, their bones lying strewn across their grazing grounds. When farmers sat down to milk their cows, they found them to be as dry as parchment, their udders drained by the ugly monster that had glided into their stalls at night to suck them dry. Where the worm lived, nothing would flourish, for the slime it secreted was noxious, and the once-fertile farmland surrounding the hill became bald and barren.

The serfs sent a deputation to the back door of Lambton Hall to inform the Lord of the Manor respectfully that as his son had introduced the monster to their lands, perhaps he could consider finding a way of getting rid of the voracious beast. "I'll do all I can," he promised as they stood together on the cobbled courtyard.

He was sitting down to ponder his problem when the neighbouring nobles dropped around and were invited inside where he brought out the wax-encrusted bottles of good French wine from his cellar.

Glass in hand, Earl Fitzmaurice spoke: "You'll have to do something, Lambton. It's your responsibility, you know! It's causing so much unrest, this worm of yours, that if action isn't taken soon, there'll be no accounting for what might happen. Why, these fellows will be asking for more money, or they'll want us to take a smaller proportion of their crops for the use of our grinding mills; and once that kind of nonsense starts, God knows where it could end. It might lead to insurrection and rebellion; and times are hard enough as it is, with the Crusades draining our money away in land taxes."

The frail old man promised to do what he could, and on the follwing day something happened to prompt him to swift action. He was in his rose garden, pruning his favourite blossoms that no serf was allowed to tend, when he heard a horse clattering at full gallop across the bridge. He looked up to see his farm overseer leaping to the ground and running towards him, hat in hand. "What has happened, Jones, to bring you here at this time of day?" he asked quietly.

Panting, the burly overseer replied, "My Lord, it's the monster! It's left the fields and has swum the river and is heading in this direction. It'll be in the courtyard at the back in no time at all. May I suggest we get some milk ready to soothe the beast?" They roused the hall servants and filled a trough with the milk of nine cows, and then they all rushed into the house and stood looking through the open windows, the servants trembling in their agitation.

They saw the monster come gliding into the courtyard, big and venomous, with its two fearsome claws coming out to clutch the side of the trough. It sank its head into the milk and in a twinkling the trough was drained to the last drop. Appalled, they watched it slithering away, its malevolent head moving before it from side to side, its fat body rustling the low-branched leaves of the oaktrees. It furrowed the ground as it went, leaving a deep and slimy trail to mark its course across the fields.

When the shock of silence had passed, Lord Lambton said, "Jones, tomorrow I want you to fill the trough again, only this time we'll have a dozen archers up here to loose their arrows upon the monster when it comes to drink. Tomorrow we shall rid the neighbourhood of this pestilential worm."

As the worm immersed its head in the milk on the following day, a rain of arrows whistled down upon it, despatched by the muscular arms of the strongest bowmen available, who were awaiting their call to fight in the Crusades. To their amazement and horror, the arrows that would have driven through a foeman—and come out on the other side—merely bounced off the monster's coils and, with a scream of rage, it picked up the huge trough and hurled it into splinters on the cobbled courtyard. Moving away without hurry or fear, it tore twelve sturdy oaktrees out of the ground, roots and all, and flung them to one side as easily as a man would throw a stick or a twig. "We'll feed it again tomorrow," said Lord Lambton resignedly, "but without the arrows. We'll have to find some other way of despatching the beast."

During the weeks in which the monster lived on the milk provided by His Lordship, it devoured no more than one sheep or one ox or pig a day, and during that time Lord Lambton had finalized his plans. Brave young knights from the neighbouring shires came to his door, attracted thither by a vast reward and the chance to sharpen up their warlike skills before the next contingent was mustered to bolster the Crusaders already fighting in Europe. They came armed with courage and training, horses and armour, double-bladed swords and their retinues of squires.

Young Montgomery Fitzalain was the first to go, a stirring sight in full armour, his lance pointing to the sky. As he galloped closer to the hill and lowered his lance for the kill, he spurred his brown horse to greater speed, and the distant spectators saw the monster's head swinging round to face the noble knight. Then the head swung away from them as Fitzalain disappeared behind

the hill. They held their breath as dust rose high in the air, and slowly settled down again.

They saw the riderless horse emerging on the other side; and while the monster was drinking the milk of nine cows from the trough in the courtyard later that day, servants retrieved the horribly mangled body of the brave young man and on the following morning nobles and serfs alike attended the burial service in the graveyard of St Mary Overbury. Within the week there were seven new graves to keep him company; while other knights, fortunate enough to survive, limped sadly home, mauled and maimed, some minus an arm or a leg.

Then two knights rode forth together, fortified by a pre-arranged strategy. One of them would lure the monster away from the hill so that its body would be stretched full length along the ground for the second knight to cut through it with his two-handed sword. The onlookers saw the plan succeed spectacularly, and a cheer went up as the sunlit blade came down and sliced the worm in two halves. But the severed parts re-united themselves as if by magic, and the tail swept round to hurl one knight from his saddle while the monstrous head dealt with the other nobleman. They, too, were interred in the graveyard of St Mary Overbury in a sombre ceremony. "The monster is indestructible," the people whispered. Fear grew, and gloom, and hopelessness.

A deputation from the serfs, cap in hand but with firm intent, insisted that Lord Lambton alone should provide milk and meat for the worm, on the grounds that his son had been responsible for its presence on their lands. Lambton Hall became impoverished and run down as one year followed the next.

Seven years after he had fished up the worm on that fateful Sunday morning, the heir to Lambton Hall returned from the Crusades to find his father old and white-haired, withered by adversity, the fields all around untended and barren and a sullen hostility directed against himself by nobles and serfs alike.

But enmity slowly gave way to admiration as the young man shouldered full responsibility for the catastrophe that his youthful iniquity had caused, and promised to despatch the monster within the week. "There is a marked change in him," all said who recalled him as he used to be. "Battle has tempered his spirit, and given him maturity and authority."

He had, indeed, become pensive, much given to spending hours on his knees on the cold stone floor of the chapel, for he had waded through blood in the years that he had been away, and had colluded in the slaughtering of innocents, and he felt an urge to beg God's forgiveness for what he had done in a cause that seemed less holy the more he put his tortured mind to it.

He rode out to survey the worm, now grown to fully ninety feet in length, its body as thick as a small barrel, its scales seemingly impenetrable, its head with nine holes along each side ugly enough to disgust the young knight who had wallowed in ugliness for seven long years. Then he trotted fifteen miles into a neighbouring shire to consult a Wise Woman of whose extraordinary powers of perception he had been made aware by the local priest.

"You alone can alleviate the misery you have unwittingly caused," she told him. "Success will accompany you if you follow my instructions to the letter. Stud your strongest suit of armour with spearblades, then take your stand—armed with sword and valour—on the rock in the middle of the river. When success has crowned your endeavour, you must slay the first living thing you see, whether it be man or beast, otherwise a curse will fall on your descendents, condemning nine generations of Lambtons to perish by violence."

Three days later, clad in his spear-studded armour, the young man prayed in the family chapel and, before he walked heavily down towards the river, spoke with his father, reiterating what he had already imparted to him and the serfs. "When I announce the monster's death with a blast from my bugle," he said, "You must release my favourite hunting dog Samson; but on no account, father, must you go with him, or before him. Remain at home to await my return."

He moved out to the rock in the middle of the river, tethered the dinghy in a hollow, and waited. There were no spectators on the bank, as none of them wished to be a sacrifice and nobody knew from which direction the monster would come.

It uncoiled itself from the hill, to slither across the ravaged fields and rustle the oak leaves before its long length slid into the water. The young knight saw its evil head moving along above the surface, with a long trail of coils humping along behind. Slowly it curled itself around the rock on which he stood looking down at its immensity, his two gauntleted hands curled round the handle of his mighty double-bladed sword. Then its ugly head was moving slowly upwards towards him.

Mustering all his courage and strength, he lifted the sword and brought it down between the monster's eyes. His hands tingled with the force of the blow, and the shock of the impact jarred along his arm and into his

65

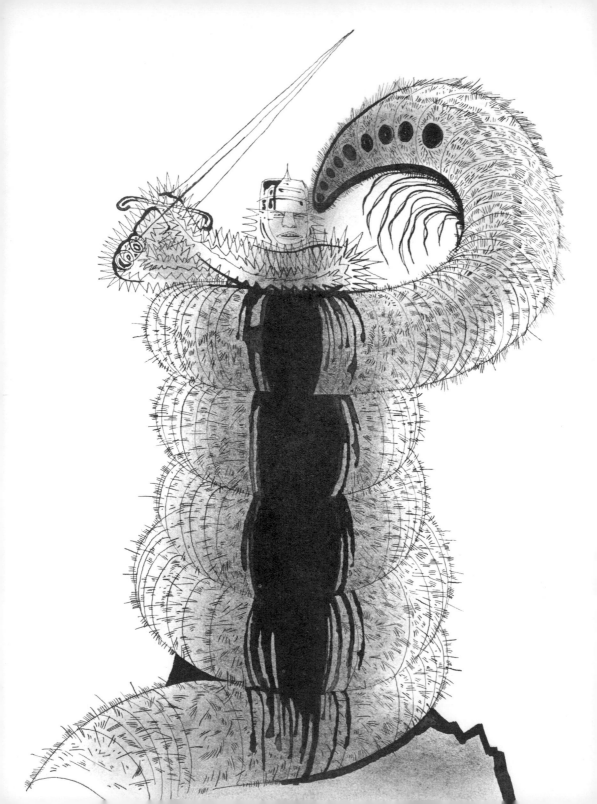

shoulders. But it had no effect on his adversary, and a tremor of fear ran through the knight.

Then the worm's head whirled past his face as its coils slithered upwards to tighten about him and all but drag him from the summit of the rock. His mind working feverishly, he realised that most of the worm was coiled around the rock below him, and only a small part around himself and, looking down, he could see the water lapping the stone stained red with blood. The spearpoints that studded his armour had impaled the monster and breached its indestructability.

As the baleful head writhed towards him, and the talons reached out to tear him apart, the worm's breath hot and stifling in his face, he began to cut through its body with swift strokes, using the sword as a saw. Bleeding profusely now, and the red stain widening about the rock, the monster's head reared away from him in anguish and, as his sword sliced through its body, the coils around him relaxed and he managed to throw them into the water.

The monster's head splashed into the river, with the severed length still curled around the rock and uncoiling too slowly to be able to reunite with that part of it which was moving convulsively in its death agonies, drifting away downstream. Then a tremor ran through the rock on which he stood, as the headless coils tightened in death before uncurling in the current, until the dead worm floated in a long straight line down the river towards the faraway sea.

Drained by his victory and drenched in the blood of the worm, he gave thanks to God, and without elation retrieved his dinghy and rowed back to the bridge, saddened by the thought of what remained to be done. He lifted the bugle, burnished by the sunlight, and blew a brassy blast that sent echoes through the still afternoon to proclaim to all that the dreaded monster would no longer be a plague to them. Wearily he waited for his sacrificial hunting hound to make his appearance.

But his face turned ashen with horror as he perceived his father tottering along the riverbank towards the other end of the bridge, unthinking in his exultation. The voice of the Wise Woman was running through the young man's mind: "You must slay the first living thing you see, whether it be man or beast, otherwise a curse will fall on your descendents, condemning nine generations of Lambtons to perish by violence."

"Go back, father!" the young man shouted as the wooden bridge trembled under the old man's steps coming towards him. "Go back and unchain Samson."

There were tears in his eyes now, and his countenance was bleak and woebegone as he thought of the future and nine generations of his family who would meet with violent deaths. And he had a deep affection for Samson, the black hunting dog that had been no more than a pup when his master had left to follow the Crusades but had welcomed him back like an old and trusted friend after he had been seven years away.

Then Samson came bounding up to him, and he killed him quickly and cleanly, resting the dog's head in his lap.

He walked slowly across the bridge towards the Manor. The serfs came out to line the path that led from the bank and cheered his victory as he moved, blood-drenched, between them. His only acknowledgment was a perfunctory raising of his hand, and they said afterwards that they had never seen a victor rejoicing less in his moment of triumph.

Brose and Butter

Scotland, whence comes the hearty porridge known as brose

With Oliver Cromwell but two years in his grave, the Restoration of 1660 revived the Stuart fortunes and brought the son of the beheaded monarch back into London from his long exile in Holland. He was crowned Charles II in Westminster Abbey: King of England and her dominions beyond the seas. The church bells clanged and clamoured all the way from St Pauls to the Abbey in Westminster as the royal carriage carried the triumphant, smiling King through the vast concourse of his cheering subjects who lined the processional route from one end to the other.

But six hundred miles to the north, deep in the highlands of Scotland, the only sound was the breeze that rustled the heather on a hill where a nobleman stood gazing out across the craggy countryside.

In his mind's eye he could see himself fighting alongside Charles Stuart at the Battle of Worcester, nine years before, when Cromwell's military genius had routed the insurgents and put paid to the ambitions of the Cavalier rebels. His blood raced as he lived again the hazardous venture that had spirited the defeated Prince away, against all odds, down to the moonlit harbour and across the sea to where the Dutch offered sanctuary at the Hague.

"It was I who lightened the burden of his loneliness," he mused, "and brightened the gloom of his exile. Gold coins were showered on the banished King by his loyal supporters—and with their help, how we gambled and drank the nights away!" In memory he swayed again across the black-chequered marble floor in the palace at The Hague, his kilt swinging, the bagpipes under his arm, and Charles Stuart reeling behind him to the skirling of the old melody that was highland and haggis, Ben Nevis and Holyrood Palace and all the glories that an exiled Scotsman holds most dear.

"Aye, I played to him drunk and I played to him sober, piping him into his bed long after midnight with his favourite air, *Brose and Butter;* and played him to the table for breakfast late the following day. Now the King enjoys his own again, while I, who was his boon companion, am alone and friendless, tramping across lands that had been mine and my family's ever since the days when Robert the Bruce smashed England's might at Bannockburn."

The Laird o' Cockpen, who had devoted eight years

to Charles Stuart in The Hague until homesickness had drawn him back to Scotland a year before the Restoration, became angry as he reflected on the injustice done him. "Because I gave my all to the Stuart cause, Cromwell confiscated my lands and property. Had I remained neutral instead of fighting for my King, I should be affluent and prospering now; but here I sit, a tattered pauper on lands that were once my own!"

He smiled grimly as he remembered the voice of Charles Stuart: "When my people call me back again, Cockpen—as they will some day without a doubt—to sit upon the coronation throne in Westminster Abbey, the very first decree I set my seal to will restore your lands to you, good and faithful friend in adversity; and the Laird o' Cockpen will play *Brose and Butter* upon his own heath again."

But the King had not even invited his old supporter to his coronation. The Laird decided to write to him, to recall the long years of unselfish companionship in exile and to chide him for not keeping the promises he had made on more than one occasion.

Six months went by without the inkling of a response from London; and anger at the King's continuing neglect so rankled in him that he vowed to carry his discontent to the metropolis and confront Charles with it in his own palace.

Too impoverished to travel by coach or even on horseback, he was obliged to take to the King's Highway, sleeping at night in open meadows—and not forgetting to thank God for that mild and beautiful summer of 1661—washing in streams and ponds and imposing upon himself the most spartan frugality so that his purse would not be empty before he reached the capital.

He was on the road for a month and more before he stood surveying London from the heights of Hampstead Heath, looking down upon the lofty cathedral of St Pauls, with London Bridge not far away, and over to his right the gothic grandeur of Westminster Abbey. He was able to find modest lodgings in Islington; and the few lonely coins clinking together for company in his depleted purse would be enough to sustain him for no more than two or three thrifty days.

On the day after his arrival, he walked through the City's teeming streets where market vendors sang the excellence of their wares, past St Pauls and across the Fleet River which ran down from Hampstead to join the Thames. He went up Fleet Street and along The Strand. By now the slums and the filth were behind him, and all around were fine mansions, horses and carriages and the ostentatious panoply of wealth. Then he walked along Pall Mall, the broad thoroughfare built by the new King, and pulled the bell sash at the side entrance

to St James's Palace which Henry the Eighth had built more than a century before.

The official who received him with cool disdain asked him what the nature of his business might be, before ordering him to wait a while. "I am within hailing distance of Charles Stuart," he thought, "and tomorrow night I shall be an honoured guest in this palace where the rafters will ring with memories of Worcester and The Hague."

But the courtier who had been summoned to deal with him gazed with unconcealed contempt at his worn kilt frayed round the edges, his shabby hose and down-at-heel shoes with silver buckles dulled by travel, and haughtily commanded the sentry on duty "to send this ruffian packing and make sure that he is not allowed near the palace entrance again."

Humiliated and struck down by this ungentle rejection, the Laird o' Cockpen walked fuming down Pall Mall into the wide thoroughfare of Whitehall, past the Banqueting House in front of which Charles I had been beheaded in full view of his former subjects thirteen years before. He stood where Cromwell's head was gruesomely impaled on one of the spires of Westminster Hall, the Protector's body having recently been dragged from its tomb in the Abbey to be hanged, drawn and quartered at Tyburn like a common criminal by order of the vengeful Charles. The Laird o' Cockpen, smarting under the sharp spur of injustice, turned his eyes away from Cromwell's skull with a twinge of sympathy for his old Roundhead foe.

As he entered Westminster Abbey, his angry feelings were subdued by the splendour of the nave, where sunlight streamed through the great stained-glass windows upon the tombs of England's Kings and Queens. His footsteps echoed hollowly on the flagstone floor before he sat down to meditate in silence. Then the organ came to life, now booming, now whispering, the deep throbbing notes pulsing along the floor beneath his feet while the high piping treble set the chandeliers tinkling above his head. "Monteverdi!" he thought to himself, "and played by a master."

When the last note had died echoing away, he heard the organist descend from the organ loft and, as the musician approached him down the centre aisle, he rose to meet him. "I compliment you on the most spendid organ playing in my experience, not only in these islands but in many parts of the Continent. I used to play Monteverdi myself in happier times, but after hearing your performance, I believe I shall restrict my future music-making to my native pipes."

Dapper in dress and warm of manner, the organist replied, "A compliment from a fellow-musician is a

76

compliment indeed." They inclined to each other immediately, as strangers in London often do. "If you wish," he continued, "walk with me up Whitehall towards my lodgings in Covent Garden, and we can converse as we go." Along the road he introduced himself: "Reginald Bryceland, Royal Organist." He listened with sympathy to the Laird o' Cockpen's recital of misfortune. Then he made a proposal that delighted the Scottish nobleman:

"Tomorrow, when I play for the King in his Chapel Royal adjoining the palace, you may care to sit in the organ loft with me. After a while I shall step down and you can play your barbaric *Brose and Butter*. We'll see then what effect it has upon the disposition of our Monarch, who invariably sleeps through *my* performances. But you'll have need of more modish clothes for your anticipated reunion, since your own outfit is somewhat the worse for wear from your long journeying. Mine will fit you well, for there is not an inch between your height and mine."

That night, in Reginald Bryceland's appartments, he felt his spirits revive, coaxed back to life by a fine meal punctuated by lively conversation and liberal draughts of whisky from the decanter that was empty by the time the evening ended.

Next morning, smartly attired and accompanied by

the Royal Organist, the Laird o' Cockpen had no difficulty entering the Chapel Royal unchallenged. While Dr Bryceland played Monteverdi, he sat next to him on the organ bench. A few moments later, in the mirror suspended above him, he saw Charles enter the Chapel, his gold-tipped stick tapping before him, black curls down to his shoulders, his moustache a thin black line below the acquiline nose. Unaccompanied, the King moved into the Royal Pew, closed his eyes and dropped his head on to his chest. After observing the King for some time, Cockpen realized that Charles was not praying but sleeping—and through such superb music-making! And he said to himself, "I'll awaken my ungrateful Monarch and the Devil take the consequences!"

"Take my place," whispered the Royal Organist, and the Laird o' Cockpen sat down to play. The organ stops flew in and out and up and down as the jaunty refrain of *Brose and Butter* whirled through the church, the high notes tumbling and dancing gleefully.

In the mirror above his head, the musician was pleased to see the King stir, opening his eyes and beating his stick rhythmically upon the floor. Over his handsome, dissolute countenance came an expression in which joy and nostalgia mingled, and then the royal brow furrowed with the pangs of conscience and the

guilt of a promise made and broken.

The music stopped, and silence crept back into the chapel, to be broken by the King calling, "Bryceland, I wish to speak with you!" The Laird watched the Royal Organist walk up the aisle and bow deeply before his royal patron.

"Who was it playing *Brose and Butter?*" Charles demanded.

"It was not I, your majesty."

"Of that I am perfectly aware," the King replied, the hint of a smile crossing his swarthy face. "You are a formidable performer, Dr Bryceland, but that ancient Scottish air is outside your spiritual range, and not even you could have played it so truly. In fact, no Englishman is capable of turning a church organ into a set of bagpipes; only a highlander could make an organ skirl *Brose and Butter* with such fervour and such glorious barbarity. Let me meet the man who has been sharing your duties today."

Trembling with anticipation, and moved despite himself by a highlander's proximity to his Sovereign, the Laird o' Cockpen stepped down from the organ loft and bowed the knee to his King.

"Stand up, man!" Charles ordered. Then, his voice softening, he said, "Ah, Cockpen, my old friend and benefactor, it *is* you, then? I could barely restrain my feet from dancing me around the church to your *Brose and Butter*."

"I used to dance myself," the Laird replied, unsmiling, "but I vowed never to do so again until my confiscated lands were mine to dance upon. I lost it all to Cromwell after I had sworn allegience to the Stuarts and sustained my King when he was but a Prince with adversity heavy upon him."

"Well said!" laughed the King as they walked towards the door, "and spoken like a true highlander— a forthright yet tactful rebuke to one who has been in grave danger of failing to keep a promise he made to a tried and true kinsman. Cockpen, you *shall* dance to the strains of *Brose and Butter* on your own lands again, aye, and all who come after you, to the nineteenth generation!"

In St James's Palace that night, and every night for the rest of that week, whisky glowed amber in the candlelight. The bagpipe's skirl celebrated Bannockburn, evoked Flodden Hill with a sobbing lament, and imparted to *Brose and Butter* a finer interpretation than the old tune had ever known before.

By the time he returned to Scotland, in a carriage placed at his disposal by the King, the upstart owners of his ancient lands had been banished to an Irish estate, and the Laird o' Cockpen had come into his own again.